The Tower of Babel

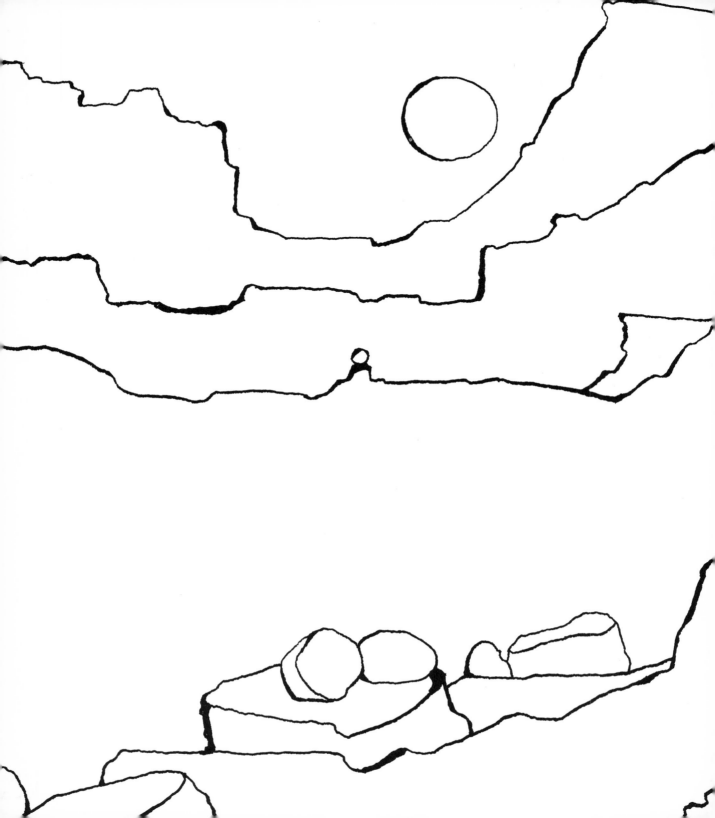

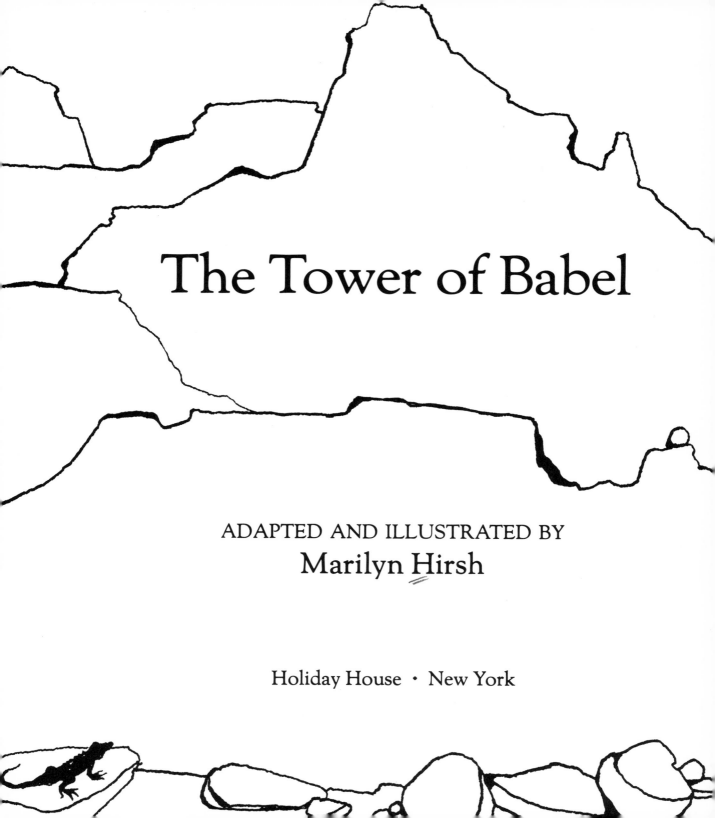

The Tower of Babel

ADAPTED AND ILLUSTRATED BY
Marilyn Hirsh

Holiday House · New York

Copyright © 1981 by Marilyn Hirsh
Printed in the United States of America

Library of Congress Cataloging in Publication Data

Hirsh, Marilyn.
    The Tower of Babel.

    1. Babel, Tower of—Juvenile literature.
I. Title.
BS1238.B2H57   222'.1109505   80-21196
ISBN 0-8234-0380-7

A long time passed after Noah, his family, and the animals had left the ark. Noah's children had children. Then they had children. Time went on and on. There were now many people and many animals. Most of the animals had gone off to find their own homes, but the people still wandered together across the land.

All the people understood one another since they spoke the same language. They traveled together like one big family.

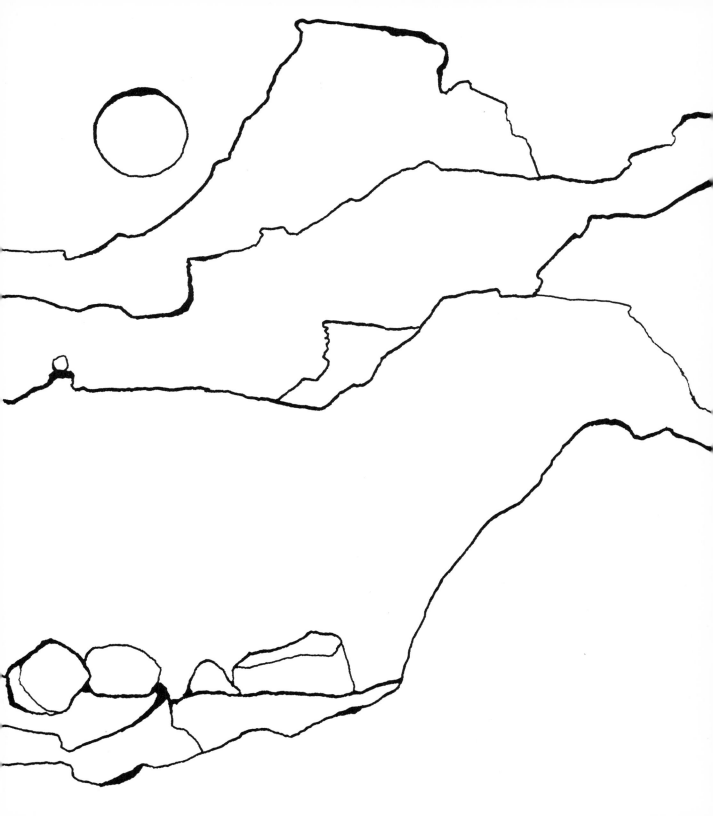

And as they journeyed east, they found a plain in the land of Shinar. They liked it there and decided to stay.

And one said to the other, "Let us make bricks from sand, and mud, and water, and bake them thoroughly. We will build a village with bricks and use mud from the river as mortar."

So they built a fine village.

Most of the people were happy with the village. They planted crops and fished in the river. They raised their families. But some people said, "This is only a village. It would be much finer to live in a city."

So they built a city with a high wall around it. It had a great gate decorated with bulls and deer. Everyone felt very proud as they came and went through the gate.

In the market place, there was the noise of bargaining and trading. In the homes, there were courtyards with peaceful lotus ponds. Most people were content. Yet, some still argued and said, "We can be greater than this!"

Those who were not satisfied called to the others, "Come! Let us build a tower with its top in heaven, and let us become famous." The people were convinced and began to build the tower, right in the center of the city.

Soon everyone was working on the tower day and night. As it rose higher and higher, everyone felt prouder and prouder.

"We must be very great to build such a great tower!" they cried to each other. "People who can build a tower like this must be the greatest in heaven or on earth."

Higher and higher went the tower. Higher and higher went the people's pride. Every man and woman worked only for the tower. It made each person feel full of power. "We are greater than anything! We can do anything!" they cried.

The market place was silent.
The crops rotted in the fields.
The lotus dried up in the unfilled ponds.
Cows were not milked.
Other animals were left to wander.
Children cried alone in their beds.
The men and women worked only for the tower.

And the Lord came down and saw the city and the tower which the people were building.

"They have forgotten their homes! They have forgotten their children! They have forgotten the Lord, their God!" He cried. "They are one people with one language, who used to live happily like one large family. But now they are building this tower, thinking they can have power over heaven and earth. I will confuse their language so that they cannot understand one another."

Soon, there was confusion on the tower.

"Give me some mortar," one man asked a woman. So she poured some water over his head.

"That wall is too tall," called another woman.

"I am not small, and I'm not going to fall," her friend replied angrily.

"Those bricks are too thick," yelled a master bricklayer.

"I am *not* sick, but maybe you are!" screamed his assistant.

Whatever anyone needed to keep working was missing, or something else was there in its place. The people were all furious with each other for not being able to understand the simplest request.

Since they couldn't work together, people began to work on their own, making up whatever design they wanted. Some designs were good but, when they were mixed together, they looked terrible. Everyone thought everyone else's work was ugly. Some people got so mad that they began to knock over other people's work. Many gave up and climbed down from the tower.

Then all the people stopped working, since they could no longer understand one another. The tower, which was never finished, came to be called The Tower of Babel. From the tower, the Lord scattered the people everywhere and, speaking different languages, they went out over all the earth.

About This Book

The Tower of Babel is found in the Old Testament in *Genesis* 11. In this retelling, Marilyn Hirsh has tried to remain true to the Biblical version. Whenever possible, she has made the language reflect Biblical style and form.

The word *babel* in the Hebrew language means "to confuse or confound." But some scholars believe that the word *babel* comes from the name of the ancient capital of Mesopotamia, called Babylon. All over Mesopotamia, people built high, stepped pyramids, called ziggurats, where they worshiped the sun, moon, and stars. One of the greatest of these was in Babylon itself. It was certainly seen by the early Hebrews and probably inspired the parable of *The Tower of Babel*.

Ms. Hirsh has chosen to draw many races in varied costumes to symbolize the harmony among all people before pride caused them to build the tower. The central message of the parable, "Pride goeth before a fall," certainly does not apply only to Biblical times. It is hoped that today's children will follow the meaning, which is, unfortunately, never out of date.

Temple Israel

Minneapolis, Minnesota

In honor of the Bar Mitzvah of
DAVID WIRTSCHAFTER
by
Dr. and Mrs. Jonathan Wirtschafter
June 4, 1983